A NOTE TO PARENTS AND CAREGIVERS

Shortness of breath. Wheezing. Coughing. Tightness in the chest. Asthma and allergies can affect our lives in fundamental ways. These symptoms can be particularly frustrating and frightening for children, who suddenly find themselves unable to control their bodies for reasons they cannot understand.

During my thirty years of practice as a physician focusing on family health issues, I have been amazed at the ability of children to cope effectively with challenging medical conditions. The main difficulty they face is one of communication. Parents—and even health professionals—often have a difficult time explaining something as complex as asthma and allergies in terms that a child can understand.

I created the superhero Katie Kate and the Worry Wombat to help capture the attention of children, put them at ease, and spark their natural curiosity about their condition and how they can feel their best. It is my hope that this tale will engage and educate you and your child and help you breathe easy as you face the challenges of living with asthma and allergies.

—M. Maitland DeLand, M.D.

Dedicated with love to my darling daughter, Claire. —M.D.

Published by Greenleaf Book Group Press
Austin, Texas
www.gbgpress.com

Distributed by Greenleaf Book Group LLC

For ordering information or special discounts for bulk purchases, please contact
Greenleaf Book Group LLC at PO Box 91869, Austin, TX 78709, 512.891.6100.

Design and composition by Greenleaf Book Group LLC
Cover design by Greenleaf Book Group LLC
Illustrations by Jennifer Zivoin

Publisher's Cataloging-In-Publication Data (Prepared by The Donohue Group, Inc.)

DeLand, M. Maitland.
The Great Katie Kate. Offers answers about asthma / M. Maitland
DeLand ; with illustrations by Jennifer Zivoin.. —1st ed.
p. : ill. ; cm.

Summary: When Julie is diagnosed with asthma, the Great Katie Kate swoops
in to help alleviate her fears brought on by the worry wombat.
Interest age group: 004-008.
ISBN: 978-1-62634-053-4

1. Asthma in children—Juvenile literature. 2. Asthma—Patients—Juvenile literature. 3. Children—
Preparation for medical care—Juvenile fiction. 4. Superheroes—Juvenile fiction. 5. Asthma—
Patients—Fiction. 6. Children—Preparation for medical care—Fiction. 7. Superheroes—Fiction. I.
Zivoin, Jennifer. II. Title. III. Title: Great Katie Kate offers answers about asthma

PZ7.D37314 Gr 2011

[E]   2011923581

Part of the Tree Neutral® program, which offsets the number of trees consumed in the
production and printing of this book by taking proactive steps, such as planting trees
in direct proportion to the number of trees used: www.treeneutral.com.

Manufactured by Imago on acid-free paper
Manufactured in Singapore, August 2013
Batch No. 1

13 14 15 16 17   10 9 8 7 6 5 4 3 2 1

First Edition

THE Great Katie Kate

OFFERS ANSWERS ABOUT ASTHMA

M. Maitland DeLand, M.D.

with illustrations by Jennifer Zivoin

GREENLEAF
BOOK GROUP PRESS

Soccer practice is Julie's favorite activity of the week. Today at practice, her coach had the team working on kicks.

Boom! Julie booted the soccer ball to her teammate and sprinted up the field.

"I'm open!" she shouted, racing toward the goal. "I'm—" Suddenly Julie felt a tightness in her chest, and she struggled to catch her breath. She had to stop running and sit down.

Her coach ran onto the field. "What's wrong?" he asked.

"I can't breathe," Julie gasped. "I think I need help. I'm worried!"

"I know you're worried. It's going to be okay," her coach said. "We'll call your parents and take you straight to the hospital."

ndrew was visiting Sally at her house. Sally's cat, Jack, sat at Andrew's feet, swishing his furry tail. Suddenly Andrew started to cough, and he couldn't catch his breath.

Sally's mother raced into the room. "What's wrong, Andrew?" she asked.

Andrew struggled to talk. "I can't breathe. I think I need help."

"Stay calm and try not to worry," Sally's mother said. "We'll go to the hospital, and I'll call your parents on the way."

Claire had just finished lunch at school. Lunch was the best time of the day because Claire and her friends liked to share desserts. Today Claire's friend shared homemade peanut butter cookies. They were delicious with cold milk!

Suddenly Claire felt dizzy. She found her teacher and asked if she could visit the school nurse.

In the nurse's office, Claire began to breathe very fast.

"What's going on? I think I need help," Claire wheezed.

"Try not to worry. It will be okay," the nurse said. "I'm going to call an ambulance now, and we will call your parents on the way to the hospital. We'll get there fast!"

4

A few days later, Julie, Andrew, and Claire waited with their parents in the pediatric allergist's office. "I'm worried," Claire said.

"We are, too," Andrew and Julie agreed.

Then a nurse took their parents into her office so that she could give them some information about the first visit with the doctor.

Suddenly, a whirlwind swept into the room! It was a girl with red hair. She had freckles across her nose and wore a long, purple cape.

"Hi everyone!" the whirlwind girl exclaimed. "I'm The Great Katie Kate. I'm here to explain what happened to all of you."

The children listened carefully, their eyes wide with surprise.

"You are all at the allergist's office because you have asthma. Asthma is a condition that makes it hard for you to breathe sometimes," explained The Great Katie Kate. "I am going to teach you about it. And I am also going to teach you how to shrink the Worry Wombat."

"What's the Worry Wombat?" asked Andrew.

"The Worry Wombat is right there behind you. He shows up when you are worried or scared. But if you learn about asthma and keep asking questions, the Worry Wombat will disappear, and so will your worries."

And with that, The Great Katie Kate gave a twirl of her great purple cape and flew into the air.

"Hold on to my Katie Kate cape and I'll explain everything. Let's go!" she called to the children.

"Look at that giant bird," Claire said. "We've shrunk!"

"That's right!" said Katie Kate. "Okay everyone, breathe in."

Julie, Andrew, and Claire each took a deep breath.

"When you breathe in, you pull air into your lungs. Do you feel it?" Katie Kate asked. They all nodded.

"Now check out the billboard. The air comes into your lungs through tubes called airways. A different word for airways that you might hear a doctor say is *bronchi*. When your airways are clear, you can breathe easily. But when something in the air irritates your airways, they swell and start to close up. That makes it hard to breathe. When you feel like you can't breathe, you are having an asthma attack. You are young, so your airways are small and narrow. That means they can close easily when they are irritated."

"So what irritates our airways?" Andrew asked.

Katie Kate smiled. "That is what we have to figure out next. And that's why we needed to shrink!"

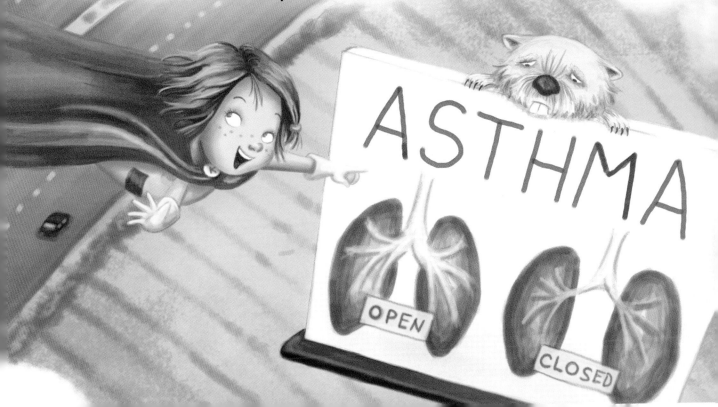

Katie Kate and the children landed in a sunny park near a bench. There was a lot of trash around the bench.

"Look at all this stuff," Julie said.

Andrew sniffed. "I can smell it."

Katie Kate said, "Grass, peanuts and peanut shells, dust, smoke, pollen—all of these things can cause an asthma attack. If something causes an asthma attack, you are allergic to it. You should avoid it."

"Is the allergist the doctor who figures out just what allergies we have?" Claire asked.

"That's right, Claire. That's why you were visiting the allergist—to find out what gave you an asthma attack."

Then Katie Kate pointed under the bench. "Look! Learning about allergies is making the Worry Wombat shrink!"

"But how does the allergist figure out what we are allergic to?" Andrew asked.

"First the allergist uses a stethoscope to listen to your lungs," explained Katie Kate. "Next she sends you to have tests, like an X-ray, which takes a picture of your lungs so the allergist can see what is going on. Then the doctor does an allergy skin scratch test."

"A scratch test?" Julie asked. "That doesn't sound like fun."

"Don't worry, it only feels like a little scratch," Katie Kate said. "The nurse will scratch your skin with different allergens. Allergens are things that cause your shortness of breath and asthma attacks. For example, if the nurse scratches

your skin with a peanut allergen and your skin becomes red and irritated, that means you are allergic to peanuts."

"Peanuts?" Andrew asked. "I eat peanuts all the time. They don't make me have an asthma attack."

"Then you probably aren't allergic to them, Andrew," said Katie Kate. "But some people are."

"Another test is the *spirometry* test. This test shows the doctor how well you can breathe," explained Katie Kate. "This is my favorite test. See, that girl is blowing as hard as she can into the spirometer."

"She is like the big bad wolf," Andrew laughed. "Trying to blow down the houses of the three little pigs."

"Look!" said Katie Kate. "I think you are learning, and that's scaring the Worry Wombat."

"Once the allergist figures out what causes your asthma attacks, she will sometimes give you medicine or shots that will make you less sensitive to certain things. See, this boy just got his allergy shot."

"Shots hurt, don't they?" asked Julie with a worried frown.

"They just feel like a pinch," said Katie Kate. "And they help prevent asthma attacks."

"I didn't like that asthma attack at all," said Julie. "I think a shot would be better."

"The allergist can do a lot of things for us," Claire said. "But is there anything we can do for ourselves?"

"Yes, indeed," said Katie Kate, nodding her head. "You can do a lot to help control your asthma. You might have to check your lungs each day by breathing into a *peak flow meter*. The peak flow meter measures how much air is coming into your lungs and how clear your airways are. If the meter says 95 percent, you are doing fine. If the meter is 50 to 80 percent, you are having an asthma attack. If you start coughing, if your chest feels tight, or if you are having trouble breathing, these are signs that you are having an asthma attack."

"What should we do if we are having an asthma attack?" asked Andrew.

"If you feel an asthma attack coming on, you MUST take action. You need to take medicine through an immediate *inhaler*," said Katie Kate.

"What's an inhaler?" asked Julie.

"It's something that helps you breathe in medicine. When you use an immediate inhaler, medicine is gently puffed into your mouth. When you press down on the inhaler container button, take a deep breath in so that the medicine goes right into your lungs, just like that boy is doing there."

"So we just have to use an inhaler to keep the asthma attacks away?" asked Claire.

"Well, children who are too little to use an inhaler or whose asthma attacks are more serious may have to use a *nebulizer,*" explained Katie Kate.

"A nebulizer turns asthma medicine into a mist that you can breathe in. You have to put a mask over your nose and mouth and breathe deeply so that you pull the misty medicine into your airways."

"You look like a robot with the mask on, Katie Kate!" laughed Andrew.

"But what if none of that works, Katie Kate?" Julie asked.

"Most of the time, if you take the right medicine in the right way when you begin to feel bad, you can prevent or control your asthma attacks."

"But if you get short of breath all of a sudden and nothing is helping you breathe better, you may need to go to the emergency room right away, just like you did before."

"When I went to the emergency room, I needed a shot," Claire said.

"And when I went to the emergency room, I needed to breathe through an oxygen mask," Andrew remembered.

"I was worried then, but I'm not now!" said Julie with a big smile.

"Neither are we!" Andrew and Claire said together.

"And look how much the Worry Wombat has shrunk!" said Katie Kate.

Katie Kate said, "To prevent your asthma attacks, you may need to take medicine every day. You might need a pill or an inhaler, depending on what causes your asthma."

"The inhaler you use to take medicine every day is sometimes called a dry powder inhaler. To use your dry powder inhaler, just breathe in and the medicine goes into your lungs. But remember," said Katie Kate, "the medicines you take every day won't help you in an emergency. So always bring your emergency medicine—the immediate inhaler—with you wherever you go. Just in case!"

"Will we always have asthma?" Claire asked.

"Sometimes asthma can change as you get older. Sometimes it gets better. You will see your doctor regularly, and she'll let you know if you need to change treatments."

"Thank you, Katie Kate," all three children said together, smiling.

"Look, the Worry Wombat has disappeared!" Katie Kate shouted with a grin. "Good job learning about asthma, everyone!"

The children jumped onto Katie Kate's great purple cape and flew back to the waiting room in a flash—just as their parents were walking out of the nurse's office.

"Andrew, the nurse said that cat fur may trigger your asthma," said his dad.

"That's okay, Dad. I can stay away from cats and use my immediate inhaler if I start having an attack."

"And I have to talk to the nurse about what I eat because a certain kind of food may give me an asthma attack," Claire said.

"And I'll have to be careful when I play soccer and take medicine from a dry powder inhaler right before I play," Julie said. "Then I can score a goal!"

"The Great Katie Kate explained it all," said Claire.

"The Great Katie Kate? Who is that?" Julie's mom asked.

"I know just who she is," said the doctor as he walked into the waiting room. "And if she's been here, I bet you are all feeling much better."

"We sure are! And we aren't worried about having asthma anymore!"

The End.